THE COUNT'S HANUKKAH COUNTDOWN

Tilda Balsley and Ellen Fischer

Illustrated by Tom Leigh

KAR-BEN
PUBLISHING

To my patient husband, Skip, with love. – T.B

Dedicated with love to Ezra and Will – E.L.F.

For Sarah – T.L.

KAR-BEN PUBLISHING, INC.
A division of Lerner Publishing Group, Inc.
241 First Avenue North
Minneapolis, MN 55401 U.S.A.
1-800-4-Karben

Website address: www.karben.com

Library of Congress Cataloging-in-Publication Data

Balsley, Tilda.
    The Count's Hanukkah countdown / by Tilda Balsley and Ellen Fischer ; illustrated by Tom Leigh.
      p.   cm.
    Summary: Grover and the Count join Aunt Sara, Uncle Joe, their children and niece and nephew, for a Hanukkah party at which the Count finds eight of many different things. Includes facts about Hanukkah.
    ISBN 978-0-7613-7556-2 (lib. bdg. : alk. paper)
    1. Hanukkah—Juvenile fiction. [1. Hanukkah—Fiction. 2. Counting.] I. Fischer, Ellen, 1947–
II. Leigh, Tom. III. Title.
PZ7.B21385Cou 2012
[E]—dc23   2011051699

Manufactured in the United States of America
1 – DP – 7/15/2012

HELLO EVERYBODEEE....

This is your furry blue monster friend Grover here. I would like to tell you about an awesome Hanukkah party we had on Sesame Street with our friends from Israel, Avigail, and Brosh.

Grover checked his list 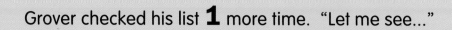 **1** more time. "Let me see..."

"Hi Grover," said the Count. "What's on that paper you are reading?"

Grover showed him. "It is my grocery list. Brosh and Avigail are here from Israel visiting Brosh's Aunt Sara, Uncle Joe, and the twins—Sam and Sadie. They came to celebrate the **8** nights of Hanukkah. Tonight is the first night, and I am doing the shopping. I bet you did not know that furry blue monsters are excellent shoppers."

onions
potatoes
apples
flour
eggs
sour cream
salt
juice

The Count read, "Onions—that's **1**, potatoes—that's **2**, apples—**3**. . . you have **8** things to buy! Oh, how I love the number **8**, ah ah ah!"

"Would you like to come celebrate with us?" asked Grover. "There is always room for **1** more."

"Wonderful," said the Count. "Aunt Sara, Uncle Joe, Sam, and Sadie make **4**; Brosh and Avigail make **6**; and you and I make **8** guests in all! **8** is the perfect Hanukkah number."

Grover was a monster in a hurry. "I will see you tonight, Count. We light the candles just after sunset."

"I will be there **8** minutes before," said the Count.

Onions
Potatoes
apples
flour
eggs
sour cream
salt
juice

Back home, everyone began getting ready. Grover and Brosh were peeling potatoes for latkes. Aunt Sara was measuring the oil. Avigail was helping Uncle Joe polish the menorah. Sam and Sadie were setting the table.

Knock, knock, knock. Who was that at the door? *Knock, knock, knock.* Sam opened the door.

"Wait," said the Count. "I am not finished. **2** more knocks make **8**! **8** is the perfect Hanukkah number."

OIL

POLISH

"Hurry! We're about to light the menorah," said Sam, pulling the Count over to the window.

Aunt Sara lit the shamash candle.

"That's the helper candle," Brosh whispered to Grover. "It lights the others."

"Can Avigail light tonight's candle, Uncle Joe?" asked Avigail.

"After the blessings," he answered.

Everyone joined hands as they sang the special Hebrew words.

"Now," Uncle Joe told Avigail. "I'll help you light the first candle."

The Count was confused. "Where are the other candles? We need **8**."

"No, no, no," said Brosh. "Tonight we'll light **1** candle with the shamash. Tomorrow we'll light **2**, and we'll add another candle each night. On the last night of Hanukkah, we'll use the shamash to light all **8** candles."

"Ah, **8** candles! **8** nights! I like it," said the Count. "**8** is the perfect Hanukkah number."

"Uncle Joe, will you tell us the Hanukkah story?" asked Brosh.

"Long, long ago," Uncle Joe began, "there was a powerful king named Antiochus. He wouldn't allow the Jewish people to pray in their own way. Many Jews refused to do what Antiochus commanded.

Judah Maccabee and his small, brave army fought for a long time. The Maccabees finally won. They were free to practice their own religion again."

"Hooray!" cheered Avigail.

Uncle Joe continued. "Now they had to fix the Temple, which Antiochus and his soldiers had ruined.

There was enough oil to light the Temple's lamp for **1** night only. But then a miracle happened. The oil burned for **8** straight days and **8** straight nights. Hanukkah celebrates the victory of Judah's small army and the miracle of the oil."

"And that is why Hanukkah lasts **8** days?" asked Grover.

"That's right," said Aunt Sara, as she set a plate of latkes on the table. "And dinner is ready."

The Count looked at the plate of latkes. "Oh no, there are **9** latkes!" said the Count. "But do not worry. I can fix this." He popped **1** latke into his mouth. "Much better. **8** is the perfect Hanukkah number."

"That's silly," said Sadie, giggling. But they all followed the Count's example and took exactly **8** bites of everything: delicious latkes, applesauce, and sufganiyot (jelly donuts). After dinner they even sang **8** verses of a Hanukkah song.

The Count set a bag on the table. "I brought a small gift for each of you!"
He counted as he passed them out. "**1**, **2**, **3**, **4**, **5**, **6**, **7**..."

Sadie noticed **1** was left over. "Who is that for?"

"Me," said the Count. "**7** Hanukkah presents aren't enough. Mine makes **8**! **8** is the perfect Hanukkah number."

"Can I go get the dreidel now?" asked Sam.

Aunt Sara smiled. "Yes, we'll all play."

The Count frowned. "Only **1** dreidel?"

Sam giggled. "Everything at Hanukkah doesn't have to be **8**."

Brosh dropped a handful of chocolate gelt on the floor and was about to explain the rules.

"Ah," the Count interrupted. "**1**, **2**, **3**, **4**, **5**, **6**, **7**, **8**. **8** chocolate coins. **8** is the perfect Hanukkah number."

"And don't worry," the Count said. "I'll be back **7** more nights—to light all **8** candles."

"Oh dear," chuckled Aunt Sara as they began to play.

After a while, Grover looked at the clock. "Count, it is **8** o'clock. Is that not the perfect time to end our totally awesome Hanukkah party?"

"Perfect," agreed the Count. And then he added, "Hip hip hip hip hip hip hip hip—that's **8** hips—hooray for Hanukkah!"

About Hanukkah

Hanukkah is an eight-day Festival of Lights that celebrates the victory of the Maccabees over the mighty armies of Syrian King Antiochus more than two thousand years ago. According to legend, when the Maccabees came to restore the Holy Temple in Jerusalem, they found one jug of pure oil, enough to keep the menorah burning for just one day. But a miracle happened and the oil burned for eight days. On each night of the holiday, we add an additional candle to the menorah, exchange gifts, play the game of dreidel, and eat latkes and sufganiyot (jelly donuts) fried in oil to remember this victory for religious freedom.

About the Authors and Illustrator

Tilda Balsley has written many books for Kar-Ben, bringing her stories to life with rhyme, rhythm, and humor. Now that *Sesame Street* characters populate her stories, she says writing has never been more fun. Tilda lives with her husband and their rescue shih tzu in Reidsville, North Carolina.

Ellen Fischer, not as blue and furry, or as cute and loveable as Grover, was born in St. Louis. Following graduation from Washington University, she taught children with special needs, then ESL (English as a Second Language) at a Jewish Day School. She lives in Greensboro, North Carolina, with her husband. They have three children.

Tom Leigh is a children's book author and longtime illustrator of *Sesame Street* and Muppet books. He lives on Little Deer Isle off the coast of Maine with his wife, four dogs, and two cats.